A Note to Parents and Teachers

Kids can imagine, kids can laugh and kids can learn to read with this exciting new series of first readers. Each book in the Kids Can Read series has been especially written, illustrated and designed for beginning readers. Humorous, easy-to-read stories, appealing characters and topics, and engaging illustrations make for books that kids will want to read over and over again.

To make selecting a book easy for kids, parents and teachers, the Kids Can Read series offers three levels based on different reading abilities:

Level 1: Kids Can Start to Read

Short stories, simple sentences, easy vocabulary, lots of repetition and visual clues for kids just beginning to read.

Level 2: Kids Can Read with Help

Longer stories, varied sentences, increased vocabulary, some repetition and visual clues for kids who have some reading skills, but may need a little help.

Level 3: Kids Can Read Alone

More challenging topics, more complex sentences, advanced vocabulary, language play, minimal repetition and visual clues for kids who are reading by themselves.

With the Kids Can Read series, kids can enter a new and exciting world of reading!

The Wright Brothers

For Gryffin Barry Anderson — may all of your dreams take flight! — E.M.

For Iwona — my safe pilot — A.K.

★ Kids Can Read ® Kids Can Read is a registered trademark of Kids Can Press Ltd.

Text © 2008 Elizabeth MacLeod
Illustrations © 2008 Andrej Krystoforski

Kids Can Press acknowledges the financial support of the Government of Ontario, through the Ontario Media Development Corporation's Ontario Book Initiative; the Ontario Arts Council; the Canada Council for the Arts; and the Government of Canada, through the BPIDP, for our publishing activity.

Published in Canada by   Published in the U.S. by
Kids Can Press Ltd.   Kids Can Press Ltd.
29 Birch Avenue   2250 Military Road
Toronto, ON M4V 1E2   Tonawanda, NY 14150

www.kidscanpress.com

Edited by David MacDonald
Designed by Marie Bartholomew
Printed and bound in Singapore
Educational consultant: Maureen Skinner Weiner, United Synagogue Day School, Willowdale, Ontario.

The hardcover edition of this book is smyth sewn casebound.
The paperback edition of this book is limp sewn with a drawn-on cover.

CM 08 0 9 8 7 6 5 4 3 2 1
CM PA 08 0 9 8 7 6 5 4 3 2 1

Library and Archives Canada Cataloguing in Publication

MacLeod, Elizabeth
    The Wright brothers / written by Elizabeth Macleod ;
illustrated by Andrej Krystoforski.

(Kids Can read)
ISBN 978-1-55453-053-3 (bound)
ISBN 978-1-55453-054-0 (pbk.)

1. Wright, Orville, 1871–1948—Juvenile literature. 2. Wright, Wilbur, 1867–1912—Juvenile literature. 3. Aeronautics—United States— Biography—Juvenile literature. I. Krystoforski, Andrej, 1943– II. Title. III. Series: Kids Can read (Toronto, Ont.)

TL540.W7M25 2008   j629.130092'273   C2007-902701-6

Kids Can Press is a **l.O⌐US**™ Entertainment company

The Wright Brothers

Written by Elizabeth MacLeod

Illustrated by Andrej Krystoforski

Kids Can Press

For hundreds of years, people dreamed of flying. They watched birds fly through the sky and wondered if someday people might find a way to fly.

Orville and Wilbur Wright dreamed of flying, too. One day, they made their dreams come true. The Wright brothers invented the airplane.

Back in 1878, Orville and Wilbur were growing up in Dayton, Ohio, in the United States. Their father gave them a flying toy they called "the Bat." The brothers loved playing with it.

Orville and Wilbur liked to build their own toys. They also built kites that they sold to other children.

In 1886, when Wilbur was 18, he was ready for college. But then, during a hockey game, Wilbur was knocked down. He hurt his head and lost his front teeth.

Wilbur got false teeth to replace the missing ones. But he still felt weak and did not want to leave home. Wilbur gave up the idea of going to college.

The brothers started a newspaper called the *West Side News*. Wilbur wrote most of the stories, and Orville printed the paper. Their newspaper was a great success.

A few years later, Orville and Wilbur were ready for a change. In 1892, they opened a store to sell and repair bicycles.

Bicycles were a new invention at this time. More and more people were riding them. Both brothers loved bicycling.

Orville and Wilbur still liked to build things. Soon, they began to sell bicycles that they had built themselves.

One day in 1896, Orville became very sick. He had a high fever. His family was afraid he might die.

Luckily, Wilbur was there. He sat with Orville every day, taking care of him and reading to him.

What kind of books did Wilbur read to his brother? He read books about flying. Some were about inventors who had tried to build flying machines.

Even while Orville slept, Wilbur kept on reading.

Soon, Orville was better. He and Wilbur began to think about building their own flying machine. They knew an airplane needed three things:

1. Strong wings
2. A way to steer it
3. An engine to give it power

One day, Wilbur was watching birds fly. He noticed that birds twisted the tips of their wings when they wanted to change direction.

Wilbur wondered if twisting the wings of an airplane would help steer it.

In the summer of 1899, Wilbur built a big
kite with two wings to test his idea. It
worked! Twisting the tips of the wings
helped Wilbur steer the kite.

Next, the Wright brothers built a glider. A glider is like an airplane, but it does not have a motor. Gliders need wind to fly.

The glider Orville and Wilbur built was big enough to carry a person. But they had to make sure the glider would fly safely before one of them tried flying in it.

To get their glider in the air, the brothers needed to take it somewhere with lots of wind. Orville and Wilbur chose a place called Kitty Hawk, in North Carolina.

Kitty Hawk is beside the Atlantic Ocean.
It is one of the windiest places in America.
It also has lots of sand. Sand would give
the glider a soft place to land.

In October 1900, the brothers started
testing their glider at Kitty Hawk.
Sometimes people helped them.

The strong winds at Kitty Hawk whipped sand into Orville and Wilbur's eyes. One time, the wind picked up the glider and smashed it back down.

The Wright brothers repaired their glider. They made changes to help it fly more smoothly.

For the next three years, Orville and
Wilbur spent most of their time in Dayton.
But every fall they were in Kitty Hawk,
working on the glider.

The brothers built larger and larger
gliders. They also tried using different
wing shapes and tails.

By fall 1903, the Wright brothers were ready for the next step. They wanted to turn a glider into an airplane.

To do that, the brothers needed to add a motor. They created a motor that was powerful and light. Then they attached it to the glider.

At first, the motor didn't work well. But Orville and Wilbur kept trying.

The winds at Kitty Hawk blew colder and colder. Sometimes, the brothers had to wear their coats, shoes and hats in bed to stay warm.

By December 14, Orville and Wilbur were ready to try out their airplane. They called it the *Flyer*. But it could hold only one person.

Which brother would get to go first? Orville and Wilbur tossed a coin to decide.

Wilbur won the coin toss. He climbed into the *Flyer*. It sped forward, lifted into the air — and crashed!

Luckily, Wilbur was not hurt. But it took the brothers two days to fix the *Flyer*.

Orville and Wilbur were ready to try again. But their airplane needed wind to take off. There was none that day.

The next day, December 17, was very windy. It was too windy to test the *Flyer*.

The brothers decided to try anyway. Winter was coming, and soon it would be too cold at Kitty Hawk. They would have to wait until spring to test the *Flyer*.

Wilbur and Orville did not want to wait. Someone else might become the first to fly.

The brothers waited until the winds were a little calmer. This time, it was Orville's turn to fly the airplane. He carefully lay down in the middle of the *Flyer*.

Wilbur held his breath as he watched the *Flyer* take off. It flew into the sky!

On December 17, 1903, Orville Wright became the first person to fly in an airplane.

Orville's flight only lasted 12 seconds, and the airplane did not go far. But the brothers made more flights that day. Each time, the *Flyer* stayed in the air longer.

The Wright brothers became world famous for their invention. They went on to build bigger and better airplanes.

It used to take days to cross an ocean in a ship. But today, thanks to Orville and Wilbur, people can fly that far in hours.

The airplane became one of the most important machines ever invented. It all started with two brothers and a dream.

More facts about Orville and Wilbur

• Wilbur was born on April 16, 1867. He died on May 30, 1912.

• Orville was born on August 19, 1871. He died on January 30, 1948.

• At Kitty Hawk, you can see a copy of the Wright brothers' airplane the *Flyer*.

• When astronauts first landed on the moon, they carried with them a piece of cloth from the *Flyer*.

Look for these other Level 3 books in the Kids Can Read series

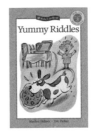

Visit www.kidscanpress.com for more information

DATE DUE